STAR WARS®

ADVENTURES

The Cavern of
Screaming Skulls
NOVEL

STAR WARS®
ADVENTURES

The Cavern of Screaming Skulls

Ryder Windham

LUCAS BOOKS

SCHOLASTIC INC.

New York • Toronto • London • Auckland • Sydney
Mexico City • New Delhi • Hong Kong • Buenos Aires

ISBN 0-439-45880-3

12 11 10 9 8 7 6 5 4 3 2 1   2 3 4 5 6 7/0

Printed in the U.S.A.
First Scholastic printing, November 2002

The Cavern of
Screaming Skulls

INTRODUCTION

The planet Fondor was famous throughout the galaxy for its orbital starship yards, where large vessels were constructed and repaired beyond the restraint of gravity. Fondor had several moons, including Nallastia. Both Fondor and Nallastia were inhabited by humans, but the environmental differences between them were extreme. Fondor's entire surface had been completely industrialized ages ago. It was covered by factories, cooling towers, and corporate offices. Nallastia, in contrast, was a lush world of terra formed jungles. The Nallastian people regarded nature with great respect.

While searching for a Nallastian interstellar freighter that had failed to return from a journey to the planet Esseles, a Fondor Space Patrol ship discovered a mammoth derelict drifting in space. The patrol ship's crew believed the derelict was the 4,000-year-old *Sun Runner*, a legendary starship that vanished without a trace shortly after it delivered the first human colonists to Nallastia. The patrol ship managed to send the derelict's description and coordinates to Space Patrol headquarters, but then the patrol ship also went missing.

The Jedi Council assigned the Jedi Knight Obi-Wan Kenobi and his Padawan apprentice, Anakin Skywalker, to investigate the lost ships alongside Bultar Swan, a Jedi Knight whose jurisdiction included the Fondor system. According to Bultar, there was evidence that the Nallastian freighter may have located the derelict *before* the Fondor Space Patrol ship. The Nallastians claimed ownership of the *Sun Runner*, but Fondor insisted that it controlled all salvage rights. Unwilling to compromise, the two worlds braced themselves to fight for the derelict.

While the Jedi attempted to negotiate a temporary truce between the leaders of Fondor and Nallastia, the derelict's engine activated and it escaped into space, heading straight for Fondor. Using a pair of borrowed starfighters, Obi-Wan and Anakin managed to catch up with the elusive ship. Once on board, they learned it contained a concealed hangar that carried the missing freighter and patrol ship. They also learned the so-called derelict was really a gigantic transport that had been disguised to look like the *Sun Runner*. Unknown to the Jedi, the transport had been secretly constructed by Groodo the Hutt, an Esseles-based manufacturer of starships and hyperdrives who schemed to destroy Fondor's orbital yards so that he might gain more business.

Obi-Wan and Anakin freed the captive ships and destroyed the droid-piloted transport before it could reach Fondor, but they became separated after the transport exploded. Obi-Wan had to bring his fuel-depleted starfighter to Fondor before he could attempt to track down Anakin, who had ejected from his disabled fighter and landed in a jungle forest on Nallastia.

Still on Nallastia, under a starlit sky, Anakin had made a small shelter and was about to go to sleep—when a large, yellow-eyed creature leaped at him from the shadows....

CHAPTER ONE

The creature was midair when suddenly, from Anakin Skywalker's point of view, it appeared to slow down, as if the beast were pushing itself through water instead of air. Anakin knew there was nothing wrong with the air or the creature's movements. It was his own speed that had greatly increased, causing everything around him to appear sluggish. Anakin's eyes swiftly took in the creature that now seemed to hover before him, illuminated by the light of the nearby campfire. The creature was a scale-covered reptile with six muscular legs and a long, lean body. Its jaws were open, and it displayed three rows of very sharp teeth.

Anakin moved incredibly fast. He grabbed the reptile's forelegs and then fell on his back as he brought his own legs up, planting his feet against his attacker's stomach. Anakin released his grip on the reptile and kicked out, letting the reptile sail through the air. The reptile's head crashed against a thick tree trunk, then its entire body flopped to the ground with an ugly thud.

"Let that be a lesson to you," Anakin said as the reptile scurried off away from the camp and into the darkness. When the creature was out of sight, Anakin returned to his crude shelter of broad leaves and retrieved his lightsaber and boots. Then he trotted past the campfire and made his way back to the jet-powered seat that he had used to eject from his CloakShape starfighter. He moved quietly through the dense jungle growth, listening for the sound of more creatures. He heard nothing.

The ejected seat rested at a slight angle on a grassy hill. Anakin crouched down to inspect a small compartment in the seat's base. The compartment housed a built-in homing beacon, which emitted a signal from its internal transponder. Anakin hoped this would allow Obi-Wan to locate him on Nallastia. The only reason Anakin had left his camp was to make sure the homing beacon was still operating. It was.

Anakin looked up at the star-filled sky. Shortly after his arrival on Nallastia, he had memorized the positions of several stars in relation to the surrounding treetops and now he noted that the stars' positions had shifted only slightly. He knew the marginal shift indicated a slow rotation for the jungle moon, but he had no idea how long night would last. Anakin was exhausted but, after his encounter with the reptile, he was reluctant to go to sleep.

Anakin let his gaze travel across the starscape until his eyes locked on a small point of light that he knew was actually the binary stars Tatoo I and Tatoo II, the twin suns of his home planet, Tatooine. There, as a boy, he would climb to the roof of his hovel at night, lie back, and imagine he was as far away from Tatooine as possible. Now here he was in the Fondor system, 40,000 light-years away from the hovel's roof, and he was imagining the day he would return to Tatooine and free his mother.

He glanced at the homing beacon again and wondered what was keeping Obi-Wan.

As Obi-Wan Kenobi piloted his fuel-depleted Z-95 Headhunter toward the starship yards of Fondor, he saw three other vessels heading in the same direction. At first glance, the three vessels appeared to be traveling in close formation, but Obi-Wan recognized the ships and realized they were actually connected by their docking ports. Of the three linked vessels, the central was the Republic cruiser *Unitive*, which had delivered Obi-Wan and Anakin to the Fondor system. The two other ships were a Fondor-based salvage hauler and a Nallastian rescue runner. Only the *Unitive*'s engines were leaving an emissions trail. Obi-Wan had not seen the three ships since they had been disabled by a power surge and he and Anakin had left to pursue the droid-controlled transport.

The three linked vessels arrived at an orbital maintenance station, where they separated at their docking ports. As the station's tractor beams locked onto each ship and guided them safely to pressurized hangars, Obi-Wan followed the *Unitive* and landed on a platform in the same hangar. As he climbed out of the Headhunter's cockpit, he saw Bultar Swan stepping down the *Unitive*'s landing ramp. Bultar was followed by Senator Rodd of Fondor, Margravine Quenelle of Nallastia, and their respective diplomatic aides. Obi-Wan removed his flight helmet and loosened the collar of his g-suit.

"Are you all right?" Bultar Swan asked.

"Yes," Obi-Wan said. "How's the *Unitive*?"

"Engines and sensors are up and running, but the deflector-shield generator remains damaged. Where's Anakin?"

Before Obi-Wan could answer, Margravine Quenelle exclaimed, "The *Sun Runner*! Did you lose it?"

"The ship was not the *Sun Runner*," Obi-Wan replied. "It was a replica, a transport with the *Sun Runner*'s markings. We don't know who built it, but it appeared to be under the control of droids. It also had a hologram-concealed hangar that was equipped with a tractor beam, which the droids used to capture the Nallastian freighter and the Fondor Space Patrol ship. I regret to admit that they captured me, too, but thanks to Anakin, we all escaped."

"Both the freighter and the patrol ship have been recovered," Bultar Swan informed Obi-Wan.

"After we got the *Unitive*'s sensor array working, we received a transmission from Space Patrol notifying us that the ships had docked at this station. That's why we came here."

Senator Rodd scowled at Obi-Wan and said, "You didn't exactly answer the Margravine's question. *Where* is the ship with the *Sun Runner*'s markings?"

"It was on a collision course for Fondor. We were left with no choice but to destroy the entire ship, droids and all."

"What?" Senator Rodd gasped. "How?"

"We set a thermal detonator to blow up the transport's hypermatter reactor."

The Margravine asked, "You're *certain* the transport was not genuine, that the droids had not been installed within the original *Sun Runner*?"

Obi-Wan nodded. "Quite positive. Its superstructure was made from new materials. The outer hull must have been deliberately distressed to appear ancient." Turning to Bultar, he said, "Anakin and I were separated after the transport exploded. I saw a second, smaller explosion over Nallastia and I suspect Anakin may have been forced to land there. Unfortunately, the transport's debris and radiation were causing interference on all comm frequencies, preventing me from getting a lock on Anakin's homing beacon. I wanted to continue my search on Nallastia, but my Headhunter was so low on fuel, it would have been a one-way trip."

"Are you certain your apprentice landed on Nallastia, and that he is still alive?" Margravine Quenelle asked.

"If he had perished, I would have sensed it," Obi-Wan replied. "Will you grant us permission to search for him on your planet?"

"Of course," replied the Margravine.

Obi-Wan turned to Bultar and asked, "How long before the *Unitive*'s deflector-shield generator is repaired?"

"The engineers say at least three hours."

The Margravine said, "May I suggest we take a shuttle that I keep docked at this station?"

"That is most generous," Obi-Wan said. "Thank you."

As Margravine Quenelle turned to one of her aides to arrange for the preparation of her shuttle, Senator Rodd commented, "I must say, she seems to be taking the loss of the *Sun Runner* rather well."

"As I said, the transport was *not* the *Sun Runner*," Obi-Wan corrected.

An unfriendly smile crossed Rodd's face. "I'm not as trusting as the Margravine is. It would not surprise me to learn that you blew up the real *Sun Runner* so neither Fondor nor Nallastia could claim it, effectively resolving our dispute."

14

"I would never deliberately damage a historic artifact unless lives were at stake," Obi-Wan answered. "And lives *were* at stake, but the fact remains that the transport was recently constructed. The tractor-beam projector was the latest model by Phylon Transport, and the hologram projector was a modified Plescinia. I saw at least three models of droids wander in and out of the hangar. They were SoroSuub 501-Z security units, and, if my memory serves, each was carrying a brand new Merr-Sonn B-20 blaster rifle with a pressure-wiped stock. That transport definitely wasn't drifting through the Unknown Regions for four millennia. More likely, it was constructed within the past four years."

"That's quite a claim," Senator Rodd said sarcastically. "I don't suppose you brought back any physical evidence to back it up?"

"No," Obi-Wan said. "By the time Anakin liberated my starfighter from the hangar's tractor beam, we had less than eleven minutes to destroy the transport before it reached Fondor. If you doubt my description of the hangar, I suggest you consult the crew of your recovered patrol ship and ask them what they saw."

Senator Rodd fumed. "For all I know, you may have employed Jedi mind tricks to have the patrol ship's crew tell me only what you *want* me to believe, leaving them even less reliable than the memory-wiped droids you say were on board. Now, if you'll excuse me, I have business elsewhere."

As Rodd turned on his heel and headed out of the hangar, Bultar Swan leaned close to Obi-Wan and whispered, "You did not tell Senator Rodd that the transport's droids were memory-wiped."

"No, I didn't," Obi-Wan acknowledged. Thinking back to the words he had used to describe the droids, he said, "The senator may have misquoted me, but I sensed he was hiding something."

"Something like the truth," Bultar said. "I sensed it, too."

Just then, the *Unitive*'s captain walked across the landing pad and handed a satchel to Obi-Wan. "Here are your own clothes," Captain Pietrangelo said. "In case you want to get out of that constricting g-suit."

Obi-Wan said, "Thank you. Bultar informed me the *Unitive*'s sensor array is operational?"

"Yes, sir."

"Then please send an encrypted message to the Jedi Council. Tell them Bultar and I are going to Nallastia to search for Anakin, and that we request backup."

The captain nodded and walked back to the *Unitive*. Bultar turned to Obi-Wan and asked, "You really think we'll need backup?"

"It's not what I think, but what I feel," Obi-Wan replied.

Before Bultar could press Obi-Wan for details, Margravine Quenelle returned to them and said, "The shuttle is ready for launch. We can leave at once."

After leaving the hangar, Senator Rodd went to one of the station's comm centers, where he entered a private address code on the planet Esseles into a HoloNet transceiver. After entering the code, Rodd faced a concave hologram projection pod and waited. Several seconds later, the holographic image of a Hutt appeared over the projection pod. The Hutt's mouth was moving up and down; Rodd assumed the Hutt was offering a salutation, but he could not hear it. Rodd adjusted the audio volume, heard a slurping sound, and realized the Hutt had not been talking at all. He had been chewing.

Rodd said in Basic, "Groodo, we need to talk."

The Hutt burped and licked his lips. "I'm Boonda. You want to talk with my father?"

"Your father is Groodo?"

"Yup." Boonda popped more food into his mouth.

"Then yes, I want to talk with your father."

"Hang on," Boonda said, then his hologram vanished, and Rodd heard Boonda call out,

"DAAAAAAAAAD!"

A moment later, Rodd was again looking at the holographic image of a Hutt. Rodd said, "Groodo, something went wrong with—"

The Hutt interrupted, "No, not Groodo. It's still me. Boonda. My father's not here right now. He should be back by dinnertime, in a couple of hours."

"Tell Groodo I'll contact him then," Rodd said. He broke the connection and the hologram vanished.

Hutts, Rodd thought with disgust. *They all look alike to me.*

CHAPTER TWO

Still awake, Anakin had just thrown another dead branch onto his campfire when he heard rustling of leaves in a nearby tree. Suspecting that the six-legged reptile was preparing for another attack, Anakin drew his lightsaber and activated its deadly blue blade.

"A Jedi!" called a voice from the darkness. "Thank the maker!"

As Anakin maintained his grip on his lightsaber, he watched as a dark-haired boy pushed his way through the leaves that dangled from the lower branches of a tall tree. The boy looked about eleven years old and was dressed in dark green fatigues with many pockets. He held up his hands to show he was not holding any weapons.

"Sorry," the boy said. "I didn't mean to sneak up on you. I saw your fire through the forest. I didn't know you were a Jedi until you drew your lightsaber."

Anakin deactivated his weapon. "I'm Anakin Skywalker. Are you a native of Nallastia?"

"No, no," the boy replied in a rush. "I'm from Corulag. My name's Klay Firewell. I came here on a zoological expedition with my parents, Tattyra and Hondu Firewell. They were ambushed by Nallastian warriors. There must have been twenty of them!"

"Slow down," Anakin urged. "Where and when did this happen?"

"Less than two kilometers from here, maybe an hour ago. I'd gone to gather berries near our landing site. There was shouting, and..." Klay took a deep breath. "I saw the warriors tie up my parents and carry them onto our ship. Five or six warriors took off with the ship, and the rest ran off into the jungle. They didn't see me."

"Do you have any idea where they might have taken your parents?"

"Both the ship and the warriors headed northeast. There's a big stone fortress in that direction. It belongs to the ruler of Nallastia."

"Margravine Quenelle?"

Klay shook his head. "No, the Skull Queen."

Anakin raised his eyebrows. "The Skull Queen?"

"That's what she's called. I've heard of Margravine Quenelle, but I think she's just a representative."

"That's news to me," Anakin confessed. He knew he would have remembered a name like the Skull Queen if Bultar Swan had mentioned it. "I regret I know very little about the Nallastians or their customs."

Klay looked confused. "Then why are you here?"

"A long story," Anakin said. "I had to make a crash landing, and I'm waiting for my Master to respond to my homing beacon. But let's get back to your situation—had the Nallastians approved your expedition?"

"Well, we'd paid for a tourist pass through the office of Fondor's senator," Klay answered. "But when we arrived in orbit, the Nallastian authorities refused to let us land. They said the senator of Fondor held no power here."

"Senator Rodd?" Anakin asked.

"Yeah, that's right. Do you know him?"

"Not very well," Anakin admitted. "Go on."

"We'd traveled so far to study the indigenous fauna," Klay continued. "I mean, we only wanted to gather data and hologrammic recordings. It's not like we were taking specimens or anything. My parents had invested so much in our ship, and the research was important to them."

"So you landed anyway," Anakin said.

Klay nodded. "I know we shouldn't have. We thought we could get away with it because we landed at night with our running lights off. We thought no one would spot us and we weren't going to stay long. We never meant to anger the Nallastians. After they took my parents, I didn't know what to do or where to go, so I ran and ran until I saw your fire. I'm so afraid of what the warriors will do to my mom and dad. Can you help me?"

Listening to Klay's plea, Anakin could not help but think of his own mother. To the best of his knowledge, Shmi Skywalker was still a slave on Tatooine. He often worried about her and wondered who would come to her aid if she were ever desperate for help. It was with these thoughts in mind that he looked into Klay's eyes and said, "Do you know the way to the Skull Queen's fortress?"

"Sure!" answered Klay. "I memorized a map of the region before I landed. I can take you there."

"No, just give me directions. You'll stay here while I search for your parents."

"But I can help you!" Klay protested. "I know lots of things about Nallastia, probably more than you. Here, watch this." Klay reached into one of his pockets and pulled out a rock. Without warning, he quickly whipped the rock over Anakin's head.

Above Anakin, there was a dull *smack*. He looked up in time to see that the rock had struck a large purple snake that dangled from a limb above him. The snake twisted reflexively up against the limb, and the rock fell into Anakin's waiting hand.

"It's a venrap," Klay said. "If its poison doesn't kill you, it'll just crush you to death."

"Maybe you *do* know more about this world than I," Anakin admitted as he stepped away from under the snake. "And even though you seem to be able to defend yourself, I probably shouldn't leave you alone out here, so..."

"You'll let me help?"

"All right," said Anakin, his earlier thoughts of sleep now forgotten. "I'll put out my campfire, then we can get moving. Just keep watching out for snakes."

CHAPTER THREE

"We're picking up the CloakShape's homing signal," Bultar Swan said from the Nallastian shuttle's comm console.

Obi-Wan had just reentered the shuttle's bridge from a small vestibule, where he had changed from his g-suit to his traditional Jedi garb. The shuttle was a combat-class Nallastian V-wing with two bulbous repulsor-lift engines. Its bridge was only large enough for a pilot and three passengers. Margravine Quenelle sat behind the pilot, turning in her seat to watch Obi-Wan move beside Bultar Swan and examine the comm console's sensor screen. On the screen, a faint blip of light was steadily blinking.

"There's still quite a bit of static," the Margravine commented to Obi-Wan. "But it seems your Padawan reached Nallastia's surface after all. However, according to our sensor readings, he landed in the foothills of Mount Octan."

"Is that bad?" Obi-Wan asked. Glancing at the cockpit's viewport, he saw that they were descending into the darkness of the moon's nightside.

"It is not good," the Margravine replied. "Many dangerous creatures live in the foothills." She ran her fingers down the collar of her lizard-skin robe and said, "This hide, for example, came from a wild grillik—a large, six-legged reptile. Grilliks are generally peaceful, but they can be extremely territorial, especially toward those who wander too close to their nests."

Eyeing the cut of the Margravine's robe, Bultar asked, "You hunt them?"

"No," replied the Margravine. "This particular grillik was mortally wounded during her attempt to prevent alien poachers from stealing her offspring. When I found her, she was in agony." The Margravine rose from her seat and pulled back her robe to reveal a bone-handled vibroblade lashed to her side. "With this weapon, I ended her pain. I wear her skin so her death was not in vain."

"Did you ever catch the poachers?" Bultar asked.

"Yes," the Margravine answered as she covered her vibroblade. "Their deaths were not in vain, either."

"How so?" Obi-Wan asked coolly.

The Margravine smiled. "Because they served as a warning to others, and we haven't had any visits from poachers since." She turned her attention to the cockpit's viewport.

Bultar leaned close to Obi-Wan and whispered, "I hope Anakin doesn't trip over any grilliks."

"I hope he doesn't move a muscle," Obi-Wan whispered back.

The shuttle descended fast, heading for the source of the transmitted signal. As the pilot brought the shuttle in low over the jungle canopy, he activated a spotlight and trained it on the tree-tops. Shooting past the trees and over a grassy field, he saw a rising trail of thin smoke. "Found the CloakShape," the pilot said. "What's left of it."

The pilot landed the shuttle a short distance from the remains of Anakin's starfighter. The shuttle's landing ramp was still extending when Obi-Wan leaped to the ground and ran toward the smoldering debris.

"Anakin!" Obi-Wan called. No answer came, but he noticed Anakin's boot prints around the crash site. From what he could see, Anakin had worked fast to extinguish the flames from the wreckage.

Bultar exited the shuttle, carrying a pair of glow rods. She handed one to Obi-Wan, then pointed to an area southeast of the crash site. "The homing signal is coming from this direction."

They found the ejected seat, and then followed a path of bent and crushed grass into the woods until they came upon Anakin's camp. Bultar looked at the small pile of dirt that had been kicked over what had recently been a campfire and commented, "It appears your Padawan leaves quite a trail wherever he goes."

"As I said, he has much to learn." Obi-Wan squatted down and placed his hand on the pile of dirt. "Still warm. He left less than an hour ago."

"And he didn't leave alone," Bultar added. "Look

here. Another set of boot prints. Substantially smaller. They lead off this way."

"Find anything?" asked a voice from behind the Jedi. Obi-Wan and Bultar turned to see the Margravine, who was also carrying a glow rod.

Obi-Wan said, "We found Anakin's tracks, along with someone else's boot prints. No sign of a fight. It appears they left within the past hour and headed northeast. Is there a settlement within walking distance?"

"Yes," the Margravine replied. "The fortress of the Skull Queen."

"Doesn't sound very inviting," Obi-Wan commented.

"On the contrary," said the Margravine, "I expect your Padawan will be most welcome there, as will we. If he has not arrived already, he will shortly. I suggest we return to the shuttle and fly directly to the fortress."

"Thank you," Obi-Wan said.

The Margravine turned to head back to the shuttle and the Jedi followed her at a discreet distance. Bultar Swan whispered to Obi-Wan, "Get the feeling she's hiding something, too?"

"Absolutely," Obi-Wan whispered back.

They followed the Margravine onto the shuttle, which then lifted off into the night, heading northeast.

CHAPTER FOUR

"Does this region of Nallastia have a name, Klay?" Anakin asked as he followed the boy up a steep incline through the dark jungle.

"We're on Mount Octan," Klay replied. "It's a volcano."

Anakin recalled that the owner of the original *Sun Runner* had been named Octan. He asked, "Is the volcano active?"

"I think it's dormant. We should be able to see it and the Skull Queen's fortress when we get to the top of this hill."

At the hilltop, they pushed their way through thick foliage to emerge before a wall made of black volcanic rock, about three meters high. Anakin said, "So much for the view of the volcano."

"We just have to get over this wall," Klay said. He spotted a vine that snaked up from the ground to the top of the wall and gave it a tug. Climbing hand-over-hand, Klay scampered up the wall. When he reached the top, Anakin was already standing there.

"How'd you get up here so fast?" Klay whispered.

"I jumped," Anakin answered. From their elevated position, they saw that the wall established the perimeter of a large compound. Within the compound there stood a massive fortress that appeared to be about ten stories tall. Like the wall, it was carved from volcanic rock. Anakin could make out staggered rows of battlements on the fortress's roof, silhouetted against the night sky. Beyond the fortress, the conical top of Mount Octan impaled the heavens. Both the mountain and fortress were bathed in a bluish glow that Anakin mistook for moonlight, until he saw its source was the planet Fondor, which had risen over the jungle to reflect the light of the Fondor system's sun. Anakin had heard the phenomena referred to as *planet light*.

"Keep low," Anakin said. Klay followed Anakin's running crouch along the top of the wall. The wall curved around a megalith and, as they rounded the curve, they found themselves overlooking a long field.

In the field, fifty Nallastian warriors stood at attention. The warriors were clothed in reptile skins and armor made from the bones of animals. Most of the warriors carried primitive energy-projectile launchers, but a few wielded relatively new blaster weapons. They all faced a woman who stood on a platform that jutted out from the fortress. The platform ended near three megaliths, massive stones that stood about eight meters tall and were separated by a distance of three meters. The three stones had been arranged in a triangular formation to face one another like looming sentries, and the plot of land between the stones was littered with bones, both human and alien.

Like the warriors, the woman on the platform was also dressed in reptile skins. Apparently the leader, she gripped a long staff that was topped by a gleaming, golden human skull. Anakin could not determine whether it was an actual skull that had been painted gold or merely a sculpture, but either way, it looked quite sinister.

The woman rapped the skull-topped staff against the platform and said, "Two outlanders have been apprehended. They claim they are not poachers, but we found evidence on their ship of their interest in the sacred creatures of Nallastia. The outlanders will now be brought forward."

An arched doorway opened at the side of the fortress. Through the doorway, Anakin glimpsed a modest starship that was parked in a courtyard.

"That's my family's ship!" Klay whispered.

Through the fortress's arched doorway, six warriors escorted a heavy gravsled onto the platform. The gravsled supported a crane with a winching mechanism, and from the winch a large metal cage dangled near the triad of glowing megaliths. Inside the cage were a man and woman who wore clothes similar to Klay's fatigues.

"My parents!" Klay whispered, tensing for a spring.

"I gathered," Anakin whispered, holding him back.

On the platform, the woman with the skull-staff faced the caged captives and said, "Do you have any last words?"

"We're innocent!" said the man in the cage. "My name is Hondu Firewell, and my wife is Tattyra. We're zoologists from Corulag. We only wanted to study the animals of your world."

Tattyra Firewell said, "Please...contact Senator Rodd's office. They will confirm that our expedition was authorized. We're sorry we landed without your permission, but we—"

"Enough!" interrupted the woman on the platform. "I tire of the outlanders and their lies." She nodded to the warriors beside the gravsled. One warrior tapped a control that extended the crane's arm, and the cage swung toward the three megaliths. Suddenly, the cage's bars retracted and Klay's parents toppled out of the cage. As their bodies hurtled through the gap between two of the three megaliths, there was a bright flash of light, and then, incredibly, the Firewells came to a stop in midair, hovering above the scattered piles of bones.

"No!" Klay shouted. Every warrior in the field turned to see where he and Anakin were crouching on the wall. Several warriors readied their weapons.

Anakin grabbed Klay around the waist and leaped just as the wall was bombarded by a hail of arrows, spears, and energy bolts. Klay gasped as Anakin landed in the midst of the warriors and then flung him across his shoulder.

Carrying Klay, Anakin sped through the warriors, dodging them before he bounded up past the glowing megaliths and onto the platform. In a single swift motion, he pivoted his body to place Klay behind him while he drew and activated his lightsaber. With his free hand, he reached out to the woman with the staff and grabbed her upper arm so she could not flee, then angled his lightsaber so it hummed dangerously near her neck. It was in this close proximity that Anakin realized the woman was probably not more than eighteen years old.

All of the Nallastian warriors turned their weapons on Anakin. Calmly, Anakin said, "If they blast me, they might hit you."

The woman called out, "Hold your fire!"

"Tell them to lower their weapons," Anakin added. Despite the fact that he was vastly outnumbered, a flicker of menace in his gaze assured the woman that he was prepared to fight.

The woman's lips trembled as she said, "Lower your weapons." The warriors obeyed.

Anakin looked at Tattyra and Hondu Firewell, who wore dazed expressions as their slack bodies continued to hover in the air between the three glowing megaliths. Anakin asked the young woman, "What have you done to the Firewells?"

"There is an energy field between these stones," she answered. "The criminals are in a state of suspended animation."

"Release them at once," Anakin commanded.

"That may be impossible," the woman replied.

Before Anakin could demand an explanation, the sound of a repulsor-lift vehicle came from overhead. Anakin maintained his position on the platform as a V-wing shuttle descended and touched down on the field beside the fortress.

The shuttle's hatch opened and Margravine Quenelle stepped down the landing ramp, accompanied by Obi-Wan and Bultar Swan. The Nallastian warriors stood aside, allowing the Margravine and the two Jedi to pass. Anakin tightened his grip on the young woman's arm and said, "Don't make any sudden moves, Skull Queen."

Unfazed, the young woman replied, "You are mistaken. I am Princess Calvaria."

Confused, Anakin asked, "If you're not the Skull Queen, who is?"

"I am," said Margravine Quenelle as she strode toward the platform. "And I insist you release my daughter immediately."

CHAPTER FIVE

"You're the Skull Queen?" Bultar Swan said with surprise.

Margravine Quenelle replied, "Only to the warriors stationed at this fortress. The rest of Nallastia recognizes me by the title of Margravine."

On the platform that extended from the fortress to the three megaliths, Anakin kept his grip on Princess Calvaria's arm. His lightsaber did not waver. Looking down at the Margravine, who stood with Bultar and Obi-Wan on the ground below the platform, he said, "I'll release your daughter after she releases her captives."

"Explain yourself, Padawan," Obi-Wan said.

Without unhanding Calvaria, Anakin nodded toward Klay and said, "This is Klay Firewell. He found me after the warriors captured his parents."

Calvaria protested, "The Firewells are poachers."

"They're not poachers!" Klay shouted from behind Anakin. "They're just zoologists!"

The Margravine then asked, "Calvaria, do you have any proof that the Firewells trapped or harmed any creatures on our world?"

Calvaria scowled. "Their ship contained many holograms of the creatures they planned to kill."

"Zoologists typically possess holograms of animals," the Margravine allowed. "Did you also find weapons and traps and cages on their ship?"

Calvaria swallowed hard. "No, Skull Queen."

The Margravine's eyes widened. "Calvaria! Do not tell me you may have wrongly accused this family!"

"They admitted they landed without our permission!" Calvaria retorted.

"That crime does not merit the Trinity Stones!" the Margravine said. "You should have simply ordered them to return to their own world." The Margravine turned to Obi-Wan and said, "I regret my daughter has acted immaturely and in haste. She has placed the Firewells between the ancient Trinity Stones, which contain a lunar gravity vortex. The stones are bound by a powerful magnetic energy field that can be entered but not escaped. After something enters the field, the stones become magnetically drawn to one another. In ninety minutes, they will meet, and then they will repel back to their original positions." She pointed to the bones that rested on the ground below the hovering Firewells and said, "Everything within the field, between the three standing stones, will be crushed."

"What?" Klay gasped.

"Hang on, Klay," Anakin said. He deactivated his lightsaber and unhanded Calvaria. "I had no intention of harming your daughter, Margravine...

I mean, Skull Queen. I merely sought to prevent injustice."

"Of course," said the Margravine.

Anakin looked to Obi-Wan, who nodded with approval. He then turned to the Trinity Stones and asked, "How strong is the gravity vortex?"

The Margravine answered, "If even one of the Trinity Stones is toppled or damaged, the release of energy could be cataclysmic to our world. That is why the warriors are stationed at this fortress, to protect the Trinity Stones."

Anakin turned to Calvaria. "Princess, you said it *may* be impossible to release the Firewells. Do you know of any way to save them?"

Calvaria replied, "It is written that the only way to deactivate the energy field is by placing the Lost Stars of Nallastia atop the Trinity Stones."

Bultar Swan said, "I have informed my companions of the Lost Stars—three power gems with auras that can disrupt magnetic defense shields and shatter force fields."

The Margravine nodded. "My ancestors, the Octans of the Darpa sector, used the power gems to raid ships and amass wealth. Four thousand years ago, Margrave Octan brought the gems to this moon, which he named after his wife. After the Margrave vanished with the *Sun Runner*, it was long rumored that the gems were still with him. In fact, he had left them with Nallastia. It was she who built this fortress and arranged the Trinity Stones, using the gems only for good. But after a gang of pirates tried to steal the gems, Nallastia hid all three in the Cavern of Screaming Skulls."

Calvaria gestured to Mount Octan and said, "In the words of our Nallastia...

Beyond the skulls that scream from walls,
The first star rests where giants fell.
The second star burns under falls.
The third star lives where monsters dwell."

The Margravine said, "For four millennia, the Lost Stars have remained in the cavern. There have been quests, but all ended in failure." She turned to Anakin and added, "Until now."

"I don't understand," Anakin said. "You think I'll be able to find them?"

The Margravine answered, "Nallastia Octan made a prophecy from her deathbed. She predicted that a ship with the *Sun Runner*'s markings would one day arrive in the Fondor system, carrying a champion who would recover the Lost Stars. I believe that champion may be you...or your Master."

"So that's why you were so eager to bring me to your world," Obi-Wan said. "But as I've already explained, the transport you saw was not the *Sun Runner*. It was a fake."

"That may be," said the Margravine. "But the prophecy did not specify that the ship would be the actual *Sun Runner*, only that it would have the *Sun Runner*'s markings. Those markings were on the transport."

Klay said, "Instead of arguing about some old prophecy, I say we get moving and find those three power gems before it's too late."

Obi-Wan looked to Bultar, then back to the Margravine, and said, "We came here to find Anakin, not to hunt for treasure. But of course we agree to find the power gems in order to prevent the deaths of two innocent people."

"Leave the search to us, Klay," Anakin said. "You'll be safe here."

"With these warriors?" Klay answered. "Forget it. Besides, I know this planet better than you."

Obi-Wan faced the Margravine and said, "Will you guide us to the cavern?"

"I'll do better than that," the Margravine replied. "It was my error to allow Calvaria to supervise the warriors in my absence, and I take full responsibility for what has happened to the Firewells. You may be a Jedi, but you do not know my world. The only way you'll find the Lost Stars of Nallastia is with the help of the Skull Queen."

There was an ugly grinding sound, and all eyes turned to the Trinity Stones. Already, the three megaliths were moving slowly toward one another, magnetically dragged over the ground by the energy that bound them. In the area between the stones, Klay's parents remained frozen in the energy field.

"All right, Skull Queen," Obi-Wan said. "Let's go!"

At this point, you must decide whether to continue reading this adventure or to play your own adventure in the *Star Wars Adventures The Cavern of Screaming Skulls Game Book*.

To play your own adventure, turn to the first page of the *Game Book* and follow the directions you find there.

To continue reading this adventure, turn the page!

OBI-WAN'S ADVENTURE: THE CAVERN OF SCREAMING SKULLS

CHAPTER SIX

After the Nallastian V-wing shuttle was loaded with emergency supplies, it lifted away from the fortress compound and headed up the mountain. Inside the V-wing's cockpit, Anakin piloted toward the coordinates for the Cavern of Screaming Skulls. Bultar Swan, the Skull Queen, and Klay Firewell sat in the remaining seats, while Obi-Wan stood braced against the wall near the comm console.

Facing the Skull Queen, Bultar asked, "When will we reach the cavern?"

"Soon," the Skull Queen replied. She turned to Anakin, who remained focused on the viewport, and said, "You're flying too close to the trees."

Suddenly, Anakin shouted, "Hang on!" He threw the controls hard to the side, and the shuttle banked sharply over the jungle forest.

"What's wrong?" Obi-Wan asked, clinging to the handgrip above the comm console.

"A flock of winged reptiles," Anakin answered as he brought the shuttle to a higher altitude. "They just came from out of nowhere. I almost didn't see them."

"It's a good thing you did," the Skull Queen commented. "They were probably migrating killspikes. Not the smartest avians, but very thick-skinned and they are able to do plenty of damage to low-flying ships."

"Thanks for warning us," Anakin muttered.

"I tried," the Skull Queen said in a matter-of-fact tone.

Obi-Wan moved across the bridge until he was beside the pilot's seat. He bent down and whispered into Anakin's ear, "I sense you're on edge."

"I'm fine, Master," Anakin whispered back.

"When did you last rest?"

"A while ago. But really, I'm fine. Besides, I could fly this thing in my sleep."

"That's not very reassuring," Obi-Wan said.

Anakin grinned. Obi-Wan returned to the comm console but kept an eye on his Padawan. Although all human Jedi were trained to function over extended periods without sleep, they still required some sleep to remain healthy. Watching Anakin's hands on the shuttle controls, Obi-Wan could see that Anakin was not as steady as he usually was. Clearly, he was tired, but there was something else. Obi-Wan wondered if it had something to do with their current mission, a desperate effort to rescue a young boy's parents. He suspected Klay Firewell's situation must have made Anakin think of his own mother on Tatooine. Anakin did not talk about her as much as he used to, but Obi-Wan knew that it was still Anakin's hope to be reunited with his mother one day and to free her from slavery.

Obi-Wan grimaced. As a Jedi, it was his duty to be a guardian for freedom and justice throughout the Galactic Republic. Unfortunately, it was very unlikely that a useless, remote world such as Tatooine would ever become a member planet of the Galactic Republic, so the Jedi might never have jurisdiction there. Obi-Wan could understand Anakin's concern for his mother, but he could not let his Padawan allow his feelings to affect the outcome of any mission. The more he thought of it, the more Obi-Wan was convinced that Anakin had taken a personal stake in helping Klay Firewell: If Anakin couldn't save his own mother, he would do everything he could to save Klay's parents. However, it was not the way of the Jedi to take a personal stake in anything. Ever.

Minutes later, Anakin brought the shuttle down on a rocky shelf that protruded out from a steep slope under the open mouth of a large cavern. As the group stepped out of the shuttle, Obi-Wan looked to the Skull Queen and asked, "How did the cavern get its name?"

The Skull Queen replied, "Millions of years before the arrival of human colonists on Nallastia, the cavern was inhabited by many native animals and reptiles, some quite large. Most of these beasts perished during a volcanic eruption that transformed their home into a series of massive lava flow tubes. Now, all that remains of them is the fossilized forms of their open jaws and writhing skeletons, embedded in the cavern walls. When wind rushes into the cave, it whistles between the bones and echoes through the tunnels and chambers, producing eerie sounds that resemble the howls of wounded, dying creatures. The sounds alone have stopped even the bravest of warriors from setting foot in the cavern."

Klay Firewell interrupted, "If we're done with the history lesson, maybe we can start—"

Before Klay could finish, the wind picked up, and a horrific wail came from the cavern's mouth. At first, everyone thought the sound was the howling effect the Skull Queen had described, but then they saw a shadowy form spill out of the cavern.

It was a spider. A very, very big one, with an abdomen almost the size of the V-wing shuttle. Each of its eight, long legs was as thick as an adult human's torso. Without warning, the spider aimed its spinnerets and released a wide spray of sticky filaments at the three Jedi and their allies.

While Obi-Wan, Anakin, and the Skull Queen leaped away in time to avoid being hit by the filaments, Bultar Swan threw her body in front of Klay Firewell in an attempt to protect the boy. Despite Bultar's effort, both she and Klay were snared. Suddenly, the spider's cephalothorax glowed bright green, and it released an electric charge that traveled through the filaments. Bultar and Klay were instantly stunned into unconsciousness.

Anakin drew his lightsaber and was about to strike the spider when Obi-Wan said, "Wait! It might have reacted defensively!"

Ignoring Obi-Wan, the Skull Queen drew her bone-handled vibroblade and jumped at the spider. As her leap carried her over the creature's back, she dragged her weapon through the area behind its eyes. The Skull Queen executed a diving roll as she landed, and the spider screeched as black blood gushed from its wound. Then the spider's legs gave out. It was dead before it hit the ground.

Obi-Wan and Anakin raced to the motionless forms of Bultar and Klay. "They're still alive," Obi-Wan said. He looked at the Skull Queen and asked, "Was it necessary to kill the spider?"

"If I hadn't, your friends would be dead," the Skull Queen claimed. "The spider first stuns its victims, then it eats them alive. Trust me...the spider did *not* react defensively."

The Skull Queen helped Obi-Wan and Anakin remove Bultar and Klay from the sticky filaments, then placed their unconscious bodies in the shuttle. "It would not be wise to leave them alone here," the Skull Queen said. "For one thing, they require medical attention. Also, there are other creatures like the spider that make this mountain their home. Some of them would be quite capable of eating through this shuttle."

Obi-Wan said, "I have no doubt that your knowledge of Nallastia is superior to ours. Are you willing to continue into the cavern?"

"I would not have come here if I was not willing," the Skull Queen replied.

Obi-Wan looked to Anakin and said, "There's a swoop and some glow rods in the shuttle's cargo bay. Please get them."

Anakin opened the cargo bay door, climbed in, and pushed out a battered swoop. Faster than any speeder bike, a swoop was essentially a powerful engine pod with a seat and handlebar controllers. Grabbing a pair of glow rods, Anakin asked. "What now?"

"Fly Bultar and Klay back to the fortress," Obi-Wan said as he pushed the swoop under the cover of some nearby foliage. "See to it that they are well treated. After the Skull Queen and I find the gems, we'll use the swoop to return to the fortress and free Klay's parents."

Skeptical, Anakin asked, "Forgive me, Master, but are you certain that is the best plan?"

Obi-Wan answered, "Given the circumstances, yes, it's the best plan. As the Skull Queen said, we can't leave Bultar and Klay here, and she has a better idea of what might be in that cavern than we do. You've already proven you can fly the shuttle, so it's best that you fly it back to the fortress. Any other plan would only put more lives at risk."

Anakin wanted to protest, to tell Obi-Wan that he wasn't afraid to go into the cave on his own if he had to. But Anakin knew from Obi-Wan's determined expression that there was no point in arguing. As he handed the glow rods to Obi-Wan, he said, "Yes, Master."

Anakin left in the shuttle, and Obi-Wan and the Skull Queen entered the Cavern of Screaming Skulls.

CHAPTER SEVEN

Entering the mouth of the cave, Obi-Wan and the Skull Queen saw the fossilized remains of many creatures embedded in the cavern walls. A cool wind entered the cave and slipped through the gaps in the ancient bones, producing a sound that was indeed chilling, like an inhuman growl mixed with an echoing death cry.

As they walked deeper into the cave, Obi-Wan glanced at the walls and said, "Could you please repeat the poem that your daughter recited earlier?"

The Skull Queen replied:

"Beyond the skulls that scream from walls,
The first star rests where giants fell.
The second star burns under falls.
The third star lives where monsters dwell."

Adjusting the light of his glow rod, Obi-Wan said, "Obviously, the first line refers to this area, and the 'stars' are the power gems. Do you know what the other words mean?"

"Only that they hint at the location of each hidden gem."

"Nallastia must have done a good job of hiding them if no one has been able to find them for more than four thousand years. But we can't let that stop us."

They proceeded through the cavern until they reached a low-ceilinged tunnel. Thirty meters later, the tunnel seemed to end in an area of total darkness.

"Keep back," Obi-Wan cautioned. Moving toward the darkness, Obi-Wan realized that the tunnel emptied abruptly over a deep chasm. His glow rod was capable of illuminating objects up to fifty meters away, and he could see a wide wall on the other side of the chasm, about fifteen meters away. He extended the rod out over the floor's edge, but the chasm's walls vanished into a distant black area. He could only imagine the chasm's depth.

To Obi-Wan's lower right, he saw what appeared to be a natural bridge, about one meter wide, that extended over the chasm to another dark hole, possibly another tunnel. He was considering whether he might be able to jump to the bridge when he felt the Skull Queen at his side.

"Long way down," the Skull Queen commented.

"And then some," Obi-Wan added. He pointed to the natural bridge and said, "It seems that's the only way across. Think you can jump to it?"

"Not if I don't have to," the Skull Queen replied.

To Obi-Wan's surprise, the Skull Queen lowered herself over the floor's edge, then stepped onto a narrow ledge, just below their position, that Obi-

Wan had not noticed. The ledge traveled down along the wall to the bridge. It was not an easy climb, but it was preferable to a long jump over the dark abyss.

Obi-Wan followed the Skull Queen, who hugged the wall as she made her way down the ledge. She was just stepping onto the bridge when Obi-Wan felt the ledge give out underneath his weight. As his hands and knees scraped down the wall, he pushed off, launching himself toward the bridge. There was an ugly cracking sound as he landed hard in front of the Skull Queen, throwing his arms out to his sides to prevent his body from rolling off the bridge.

"Are you all right?" the Skull Queen asked.

"More or less," Obi-Wan said as he picked himself up from the bridge. Peering over its edge to the darkness below, he suppressed an involuntary shudder.

The Skull Queen said, "It sounded like you broke something."

"I did," Obi-Wan admitted. "Two ribs."

The Skull Queen winced. "Do Jedi...that is, do you feel pain?"

"Yes," Obi-Wan said evenly. "But we can control it." Without further explanation, he motioned for the Skull Queen to follow him over the bridge. They were halfway across when Obi-Wan heard a *click* from the wall behind him. He spun to look past the Skull Queen to a small area of the chasm wall where a panel had slid back to reveal a round hole.

"Duck!" Obi-Wan shouted as he reached for his lightsaber.

The Skull Queen dropped, throwing herself down against the bridge, just as there was a loud burst of blaster fire, and three energy bolts launched from the hole in the wall. Obi-Wan's lightsaber was already blazing as the energy bolts reached his position, and he swung hard at them. He batted the first two at the chasm wall and sent the third straight back to the hole, causing a small explosion.

The sound of blaster fire echoed across the chasm, then died. The Skull Queen pushed herself up. "What happened?"

Obi-Wan pointed to the wall behind her, where smoke was pouring out of the shattered hole. "It was an old automated laser trap, a concealed wall-mounted laser projector. My guess is it was equipped with a sensor to make it fire at anyone who was halfway across the bridge. Do you know if Nallastia Octan installed such traps throughout the cavern?"

"I don't know. It is possible she did so to protect the power gems from pirates. I suspect that if one were to travel to the bottom of this chasm, one would find the remains of many ill-fated treasure hunters."

After crossing the bridge to the other side of the chasm, Obi-Wan and the Skull Queen entered a tunnel that delivered them to a high-ceilinged chamber. To their amazement, the chamber's walls were lined with enormous statues of alien beings, some standing more than eight meters high. If the statues were faithful likenesses, the beings were insectlike creatures with four arms and two multi-faceted eyes.

Obi-Wan asked, "Ever seen anything like this on Nallastia?"

"Never," answered the Skull Queen.

"They're quite ancient," Obi-Wan observed. "They probably predate the arrival of human colonists."

"You mean, an alien civilization once existed on this moon?"

"It depends on how you look at it," Obi-Wan said. "From their perspective, your people are the aliens."

There were fourteen statues in all, twelve of which stood upright; the remaining two lay across the floor, broken into many pieces. At first, Obi-Wan suspected the shattered pair might have been deliberately toppled, but then he noticed a wide, heaving crack in the chamber's floor, right under the area where the two fallen statues once stood. It appeared that an earthquake might have been to blame for bringing down the statues.

"I wonder what happened to them," the Skull Queen said, marveling at the statues. "The aliens, that is. Did they die off? Or move to another world?"

"I have no idea, but it would be hard to miss them," Obi-Wan said. He looked past the statues to a doorway that appeared to be a passage to another chamber. Then he looked back at the two fallen statues, and the words came to him. He said aloud, *"The first star rests where giants fell."*

"Could this be it?" asked the Skull Queen.

"Let's see," Obi-Wan said, and moved to the wide crack in the floor. Upon closer inspection, the crack opened up into a gaping hole. Extending his glow rod, Obi-Wan peered down into the hole, but instead of seeing a gem, he found himself gazing into the golden eyes of a large serpent.

Hisssssssssssss!

CHAPTER EIGHT

The serpent sprang up through the hole with its wide jaws open, baring long fangs, causing Obi-Wan to step backward and stumble on a stone. The serpent reared its head, flicked its tongue, and prepared to swallow Obi-Wan whole. This time, Obi-Wan did not hesitate to question whether the creature was reacting in self-defense. He drew his lightsaber and prepared to strike, but a stone suddenly sailed over his head and traveled straight into the serpent's mouth. Carrying the unexpected weight of the stone, the serpent's head fell back, slamming hard against the floor. The snake's body trembled once, then went still.

Obi-Wan turned to see the Skull Queen behind him. She was brushing dust from her hands.

"Nice throw," Obi-Wan said.

"I missed," the Skull Queen confessed. "I was aiming for its nose."

Obi-Wan and the Skull Queen wrapped their arms around the snake's body and dragged it all the way out of the hole in the floor. Inside the hole, they found a beautiful blue gem.

"The first star!" gasped the Skull Queen, as she removed the power gem from the hole. She handed it to Obi-Wan, who put it in his backpack.

Obi-Wan said, "One down, two to go."

Leaving the chamber of statues, Obi-Wan and the Skull Queen moved on to the next passage, which was lined with smooth walls made of a strong, highly reflective alloy. The ceiling appeared to be constructed from the same material. With their reflective quality, the ceiling and walls intensified the light of the glow rods so much that it was hard to see.

The two explorers dimmed their glow rods and moved forward through the passage, leaving a trail of footprints on the dusty floor. Soon, they were startled to see two shadowy humanoid figures—also carrying glow rods—approaching from the other direction. They quickly realized that these approaching figures were only their own reflections on a metal wall where the passage made a right-angle turn.

Following this turn, they soon arrived at another, and then another and another. The combination of the walls' reflective surfaces and the numerous turns served to confuse even Obi-Wan's sense of direction, leaving them both uncertain of which way they were heading. After several more turns, the passage ended at a metal door that was made of the same alloy as the walls.

A slender lever appeared to be the door's opening mechanism. Obi-Wan pressed down on the lever and heard a *clack*, but the door did not open.

"It's jammed," Obi-Wan said.

The Skull Queen asked, "Can you use your lightsaber to cut through it?"

"Possibly," Obi-Wan said as he held his glow rod closer to the door to inspect the lever. "But with all these reflections, I'd have a hard time seeing what I was doing." He stepped back from the door, then launched a powerful kick that landed just below its lever. The door flew open.

Impressed, the Skull Queen whistled, then asked, "How are your ribs?"

"Still inside me," Obi-Wan replied.

Passing through the open doorway, they entered a ten-sided chamber with a dust-free grated floor and ten mirrored walls. On each wall, there was a closed door, except for the open doorway behind them, which led back the way they had come. But as they moved to the center of the chamber, they heard a *slam* and turned to see that the door behind them had closed automatically.

All of the doors were identical, without any marks to distinguish one from another, and were made of the same reflective alloy as the walls. The only source of light was from the two glow rods, and all the reflections were disorienting to Obi-Wan and the Skull Queen. Hoping to regain his bearings, Obi-Wan considered marking the door through which they had entered, but then he realized he could no longer identify even *that* one. The dust-free floor prevented him from retracing his footsteps.

Obi-Wan looked down at the grated floor, then peered through the small, open gaps between the lattices. It looked like there was a stone-walled chamber about three meters below their position, but Obi-Wan could not see if it led to another passage.

"It's bad enough that I feel completely lost," the Skull Queen admitted, "but this room is making me sick to my stomach."

"Close your eyes," Obi-Wan said. "And take my hand."

The Skull Queen closed her eyes, took Obi-Wan's hand, and followed him as he stepped toward a door. "Do you know which way you're going?" she asked.

"Out of here, I hope," he answered. He followed his sense of the Force and reached out to push a door open, but his hand met empty air. He realized he had tried to open a reflection of a door. Moving slowly forward, his fingers met with a real door, and he pushed it.

The Skull Queen, her eyes still closed, heard the door open. "What do you see?"

"More mirrors," he said. He closed the door and edged his way over to another, which he opened.

"What now?" the Skull Queen asked.

"A spiral stairway," Obi-Wan said. "It goes down."

"What are the walls in here like?"

"You might want to keep your eyes closed."

Hand in hand, they descended the staircase, which brought them to a stone-walled chamber that was directly below the grated floor of the decagonal chamber they had just left. Obi-Wan saw another passage on the other side of the lower chamber and led the Skull Queen through it. As they walked, Obi-Wan said, "You can open your eyes now."

The Skull Queen opened her eyes. "Stone walls," she said. "What a relief."

"I agree," Obi-Wan said. "You can let go of my hand now."

"But I *like* holding your hand," the Skull Queen said.

"Oh," Obi-Wan replied. He didn't know what else to say.

They kept walking.

CHAPTER NINE

The passage led Obi-Wan and the Skull Queen to the largest chamber yet, a cavern with well-preserved natural features. The only evidence of an ancient alien presence was a timeworn path that weaved around the many stalagmites that rose from the floor. Long stalactites dangled from the high ceiling, and Obi-Wan imagined that one might have a similar view from inside the jaws of a gigantic carnivorous animal.

"I think I need my hand back," Obi-Wan said.

"You think?" said the Skull Queen.

"Yes," Obi-Wan said. "I draw my lightsaber with that hand."

"Too bad you're not ambidextrous!" said the Skull Queen, releasing her hold.

Their glow rods cast bizarre shadows as they walked quietly along the path. The sound of dripping water reached Obi-Wan's ears, but because of the numerous formations of stone that surrounded him, the sound seemed to echo in all directions, and he was unable to pinpoint its origin. But when the path rounded a towering stalagmite, Obi-Wan and the Skull Queen emerged at the edge of a subterranean lake. There, Obi-Wan saw the source of the sound: Water was dripping from the smooth edge of a wide, sloping stone that extended from a wall and jutted out over the lake.

Each drip sent a gentle ripple across the lake's

surface. By the light of the two glow rods, the water was so clear that Obi-Wan could easily see multicolored rocks that rested at the bottom of the basin. Looking at the smooth edge of the wide stone from which the water dripped, he suspected the stone may have been contoured by a waterfall over the course of many centuries.

"*The second star burns under falls,*" said the Skull Queen.

"I was just thinking the same thing," Obi-Wan said.

Keeping their eyes on the area of the lake below the smooth-edged, overhanging stone, Obi-Wan and the Skull Queen moved their glow rods behind a nearby stalactite so that the lake was once again in darkness. Under the water's surface, at the bottom of the basin, a glowing red gem became visible among the multicolored rocks.

"I'll dive for it," said the Skull Queen, and began to remove her reptile-skin robe.

"Wait," Obi-Wan said. "There's another way." He raised his right hand and gestured at the water. While the Skull Queen watched in awe, Obi-Wan used the Force to reach out to the submerged power gem. The gem rose up through the clear water, broke the surface, then traveled through the air and into Obi-Wan's waiting hand.

The Skull Queen said, "If I hadn't seen it, I

wouldn't believe—" Her words were interrupted by a violent splash. Both she and Obi-Wan were suddenly seized by a vitreous-bodied aquatic creature with long tentacles. Because its skin was almost entirely transparent, they never saw it coming.

The beast yanked the Skull Queen underwater. Obi-Wan—still holding the red power gem—drew his lightsaber with his free hand and lashed out at the creature's flexible appendages. The creature rolled, coughing up air bubbles, and threw the Skull Queen back at Obi-Wan, who deactivated his lightsaber just in time to catch her. As the wounded creature slipped off into the dark waters, the Skull Queen said, "I do believe you just saved my life."

"I don't suppose you have anything called a 'life debt' on this world?" Obi-Wan asked.

"A what?"

"Never mind."

The Skull Queen noticed Obi-Wan's lightsaber in his left hand and commented, "You said you drew your lightsaber with your other hand."

"Yes, well...usually." Obi-Wan clipped the lightsaber to his belt, then placed the red power gem in his backpack.

The pair left the subterranean lake and returned to the walkway that weaved between the many stalactites. They soon arrived at a passage that featured engraved hieroglyphics, pictures and symbols that illustrated the history of the ancient insectoid civilization that constructed the underground chambers. One sequence of hieroglyphs showed the insectoids welcoming a starship that carried humanoids, followed by the insectoids inviting the humanoids to a grand banquet; at the banquet, the insectoids revealed their true nature when they rounded up their guests and prepared them as the main course. In sickening detail, the hieroglyphs showed the monstrous creatures devouring all the humanoids.

Looking at the hieroglyphs, Obi-Wan contemplated the poem that hinted at the location of each power gem. *The third star lives where monsters dwell.* He wondered if the monsters were living creatures that might have survived through the ages, or if "monsters" was symbolic, like the "giants" of the clue for the first star.

Hoping they wouldn't encounter any real, living monsters, Obi-Wan and the Skull Queen continued walking through the passage until they entered another spacious subterranean chamber with stalactites dangling from the ceiling. At the chamber's center, a transparisteel case enclosed a pedestal, on which rested a green power gem. The enclosed pedestal was ringed by three stone statues of tall insectoids.

The Skull Queen said, "If those statues are the 'monsters' mentioned in the poem, it seems we won't have to worry about them."

"Perhaps," Obi-Wan allowed. "But the poem didn't mention any of the other creatures we've already encountered, so let's stay alert."

Loose stones lined a walkway that curved around the transparisteel case and led to another dark passage. Stepping past the stones, Obi-Wan moved closer to the case. As its name implied, transparisteel was transparent metal, a material typically used for viewports on starships. Although transparisteel was generally quite strong, it was not impervious to lightsabers.

While the Skull Queen watched, Obi-Wan activated his lightsaber and made a circular cut in the side of the case. When he was done, he deactivated his lightsaber, punched the circular cut of transparisteel to create a hole, and reached through it to remove the green power gem.

Still standing beside the transparisteel case, Obi-Wan was about to place the green gem in his backpack when he heard a loud *hum*. Before he could move away from the case, a force field surrounded his position, trapping him in the center of the circular chamber.

"Another trap?" the Skull Queen asked.

"It seems Nallastia Octan installed a force field

as additional protection for this power gem," Obi-Wan surmised. "I think the field was activated when I removed the gem from its pedestal."

"But the power gems have auras that can shatter force fields," the Skull Queen said. "Since you have the gems, you should be able to walk straight through the field."

Obi-Wan held the green gem out before him and took a cautious step forward. There was a loud crackling sound as the force field was disrupted, and Obi-Wan walked safely away from the transparisteel case. "Amazing," he said as he joined the Skull Queen near the three stone statues.

Suddenly, the three statues began to tremble. Obi-Wan and the Skull Queen backed away. To their astonishment, the statues suddenly burst open like exploding shells, revealing the bodies of three giant insectoid creatures that had been concealed within.

Standing amidst the rubble of their containers, the three insectoids were virtually identical, each with four claw-tipped arms and two multifaceted eyes. One was slightly taller and had a wider head. All three turned to look at Obi-Wan and the Skull Queen.

The insectoids were alive.

CHAPTER TEN

"I thought they were just statues!" the Skull Queen yelled.

"So did I," Obi-Wan yelled back. "It seems they were coated with a layer of stone, an envelope to keep them in a state of suspended animation. Perhaps the energy released by the force field somehow caused the envelopes to crumble."

Before the Skull Queen could comment on Obi-Wan's theory, the tallest insectoid's mandibles retracted, and it let out a shrill shriek. Obi-Wan sensed the shriek was a command, and was not surprised when the two shorter insectoids raised their claws and lurched toward him and the Skull Queen.

"It's us or them," the Skull Queen shouted.

"I'll take the one on the left," Obi-Wan yelled back. "Go for their heads." His lightsaber blazed out at the same time the Skull Queen reached for her vibroblade.

Following Obi-Wan's instruction, the Skull Queen faced the insectoid on the right. The creature took a swipe at her with its nasty claws, but the Skull Queen reacted with amazing speed, swinging her arm out and plunging the vibroblade through the insectoid's neck. The insectoid's head separated neatly from its body, but its arms reflexively lashed out, knocking the Skull Queen across the chamber.

As the Skull Queen crashed to the floor near the entrance to the next passage, the other attacking insectoid pounced at Obi-Wan, but the Jedi ducked and brought his lightsaber up behind him. As the insectoid's leap carried its body over Obi-Wan's back, Obi-Wan twisted the lightsaber's blade through the creature's neck, then dragged it through the length of the insectoid's hurtling form. The insectoid's halved body flopped to the floor, and its head bounced off the wall with a horrid *splat*.

Obi-Wan turned to see the remaining insectoid move toward the fallen Skull Queen. Above the tall insectoid's position, a heavy stalactite was suspended from the ceiling. Obi-Wan instinctively calculated the distance between him and the stalactite, then threw his activated lightsaber high. Spinning through the air, the lightsaber's blade sliced through the stalactite just below the area where it met the ceiling. The insectoid heard the hum of the lightsaber and the *snap* of rock overhead, and looked up. The last thing its multifaceted eyes saw was the pointed stalactite plummeting toward its body.

Obi-Wan retrieved his lightsaber, then ran to the Skull Queen and asked, "Are you all right?"

"More or less," mumbled the Skull Queen.

"Come on, then," Obi-Wan said, helping the Skull Queen to her feet. "Klay Firewell's parents will be in worse shape than us if we don't deliver these gems to the fortress." Feeling a breeze in the air, Obi-Wan added, "This way."

Obi-Wan and the Skull Queen traveled through the next passage until they emerged at a small opening that was partially obstructed by overgrown weeds. Obi-Wan pushed his way through them and felt some relief to look up and see the starlit sky of Nallastia. Following him out into the night, the Skull Queen took a deep breath of fresh air.

Incredibly, they were not far from the entrance to the Cavern of Screaming Skulls. Obi-Wan pulled the swoop out from its foliage cover. He was about to tell the Skull Queen to climb on behind him when she scrambled up over the machine, threw one leg onto the engine pod, and grabbed the controls. She said, "If you don't mind, I'll drive."

Obi-Wan sat behind the Skull Queen and wrapped his arms around her waist. The Skull Queen gunned the engine, and the swoop launched off into the night. Bringing the swoop up to a cruising altitude, the Skull Queen steered over the trees and down the mountainside, heading back to the fortress.

Anakin was waiting for them. He stood near the Trinity Stones and watched the swoop's descent.

In the time that had passed, the Trinity Stones had closed to a distance of less than two meters from one another, and the forms of Tattyra and Hondu Firewell—still suspended in the air between the megaliths—remained motionless, apparently unaware of the fact they were mere minutes away from being crushed to death. Below their floating bodies, the shattered bones of previous victims had been pushed together into a high heap.

The Skull Queen brought the swoop down over the nearest megalith. Obi-Wan reached into his backpack, removed one of the three power gems, and placed it on top of the tallest standing stone.

"Where are Bultar and Klay?" Obi-Wan called out from the back of the swoop.

"They're still inside the shuttle," Anakin called back. "They're fine."

"And my warriors?" the Skull Queen asked as she steered the swoop to the next megalith.

"They're in the fortress with Princess Calvaria," Anakin answered as Obi-Wan placed a power gem atop the next stone. Without concealing his resentment, Anakin added, "Apparently, they didn't have any problem sending innocent people to their deaths, but they couldn't bring themselves to actually watch the Firewells die."

"The warriors were only following my daughter's orders," the Skull Queen replied as she piloted the swoop to the final stone. "I assure you, Calvaria will never make this mistake again."

"That does it," Obi-Wan said as he placed the third power gem on the last megalith. Suddenly, the air was filled with a dull whine. Then the three megaliths began to move slowly away from one another, and the Firewells floated down to rest upon the high pile of bones.

Anakin stepped between the megaliths. "It worked!" he shouted with delight. "The force field is down!"

The Firewells were saved.

At this point, readers who chose to follow the adventure in the *Star Wars Adventures Game Book* can return to *The Cavern of Screaming Skulls*.

CHAPTER ELEVEN

"You're sure you and your parents are all right, Klay?" Anakin asked after Tattyra and Hondu had been retrieved and revived.

"I just have a headache," Klay replied. "The Nallastian doctor said I'll be back to normal in a few hours. My mom and dad are both OK, too."

Anakin and Klay stood beside the Firewell family's starship in an open courtyard behind the walls of the Skull Queen's fortress. Klay and his parents had recovered quickly after their respective ordeals and had accepted apologies from Princess Calvaria. Although the Skull Queen had invited the zoologists to remain at her fortress as her honored guests, the Firewells had decided to leave Nallastia.

Anakin said, "I hope you have a safe flight back to Corulag."

"Thanks again for everything, Anakin. If you hadn't helped out, my parents would have been killed," said Klay.

"It was my Master and the Skull Queen who brought the power gems back from the cavern," Anakin noted. "I didn't do anything."

"That's not true!" Klay said. "You were the one who convinced everyone that my parents weren't poachers. Also, you were ready to fight all of the Nallastian warriors to save my parents. I mean, you didn't even *know* me, but you really came through. I'll never forget that."

Anakin smiled. "I'm glad everything turned out all right, Klay."

Just then, Tattyra and Hondu Firewell appeared at the top of their starship's landing ramp. Tattyra Firewell said, "We're all set to go home, Klay."

"Okay, Mom," Klay said.

Anakin looked at the smile on Klay's mother's face. He could not help but think of his own mother and how much he missed her. As he shook Klay's hand, said good-bye, and watched the Firewells leave on their starship, he almost wished that he— like them—had the freedom to go where he chose. Unfortunately, Jedi did not have that freedom. Anakin kept his eyes on the starship until it vanished into the starlit sky. He felt empty. And lost.

Obi-Wan, Bultar Swan, and the Skull Queen entered the courtyard and found Anakin looking up at the stars. Hearing his friends approach, Anakin turned and said, "The Firewells are gone."

"After all they went through, even I can understand why they were eager to leave," the Skull Queen admitted. "I hope they know our apologies were sincere."

"They might have been more convinced if they had been allowed to land on Nallastia in the first place," Anakin commented. He knew his comment had attracted Obi-Wan's stern gaze, but he continued, "According to Klay Firewell, his parents had paid for a tourist pass through the office of Senator Rodd."

"Then they were misled and cheated," the Skull Queen responded. "Fondor representatives are not entitled to issue tourist passes for Nallastia."

Anakin said, "Then perhaps something is rotten on Fondor."

The Skull Queen smiled. "I've been saying that for years."

"The Nallastians have invited us to stay for the night," Obi-Wan informed Anakin. "I believe we could all use a rest, so I've accepted."

"My cooks are preparing a sumptuous meal," the Skull Queen said. "Come. The night is young."

Anakin said, "I do not wish to appear disrespectful, Your Highness, but I regret I am truly exhausted. If I may, I would prefer to get some rest now."

"Of course," said the Skull Queen. "Allow me to show you to your chambers."

As Anakin left the courtyard with the Skull Queen, Bultar leaned close to Obi-Wan and asked, "Have you transmitted another message to the Jedi Council?"

"No," Obi-Wan replied.

"So our backup should still be on the way?"

"Yes."

"Good," Bultar said. "Because I have a feeling that this mission isn't over and we may still need help."

"And I have a feeling Anakin is right," Obi-Wan added. "Something *is* rotten on Fondor."

Still on the space station orbiting Fondor, Senator Rodd returned to the comm station and made another attempt to contact Groodo via the HoloNet transceiver. After entering the code for Groodo's address, Rodd faced the concave hologram projection pod and waited. Seconds later, the holographic image of a Hutt's head appeared over the projection pod.

"Evening, Senator," drawled the Hutt. "My son told me you wanted to talk. How are things in the Fondor system?"

"Well, Groodo, we experienced an interesting event earlier today," the Senator said, choosing his words carefully. "Some Jedi destroyed a most unusual derelict starship."

"WHAT?!" Groodo bellowed. "Destroyed?!"

Before Groodo could continue, Senator Rodd said, "Yes, that's right. I'd like to tell you all about it, but this line may not be secure. I was hoping you might be able to come to Fondor and —"

"Fondor?" Groodo exclaimed. "You mean, Fondor *wasn't* destroyed?"

"Of course Fondor wasn't destroyed," Rodd snapped, wishing Groodo would just keep his mouth shut before he blurted out all the details of their secret plan. "I said a *derelict* was destroyed, Groodo. We must have a bad connection. I suggest you come to Fondor at once."

"Sure, I hear you," Groodo replied. "I'll be on my way as soon as you're done talking. You done yet?"

"Not quite," Rodd said. "I think you should know there's still a chance we can fulfill our business arrangement. It might be a good idea if you brought some of your special droids with you."

"Droids?" Groodo repeated. "How many?"

"As many as you can," Rodd said, and broke the connection.

Rodd stepped away from the comm station and went to a viewport. He could see Nallastia suspended against the starscape and he realized he was clenching his teeth so hard that his jaw ached.

He hoped the Jedi were having a wretched time on Nallastia.

In the Skull Queen's fortress, Obi-Wan and Bultar Swan were seated at a long wooden table with the Skull Queen, Princess Calvaria, and two dozen Nallastian warriors. As servants cleared away plates and refilled goblets, Obi-Wan faced the Skull Queen and said, "Now that you have the three power gems, what will you do with them?"

"I'm not certain," the Skull Queen replied. "But I think the first thing I will do is deny any knowledge that they have been recovered."

"Why?" Bultar asked.

"Because their value is immeasurable, and they will attract the worst sort of attention," the Skull Queen answered. "I would be content if every pirate and treasure hunter in the galaxy thought the power gems were nothing more than a legend, and therefore not bother to trample across my planet."

Obi-Wan suggested, "Then it might be best if you put the gems back in the Cavern of Screaming Skulls."

The Skull Queen beamed. "Yes, that would discourage anyone from trying to obtain them. You are wise, Jedi." She turned to her daughter and asked, "Is he not wise, Calvaria?"

"He is very wise, Mother," Calvaria replied without looking up from her plate.

"A toast!" the Skull Queen exclaimed as she pushed back her chair. Rising to her feet, she lifted her goblet and said, "To the courageous Jedi who recovered the Lost Stars of Nallastia, and who has proposed that they be returned to their hiding place. He is not only an adventurer, but a preservationist as well. Three cheers!"

As the gathered warriors roared heartily, Obi-Wan looked at Bultar, who also raised her goblet to him. Obi-Wan grimaced. He did not enjoy feeling like a public display.

After the cheering subsided, the Skull Queen said, "Indeed, let no one deny that Obi-Wan Kenobi is the champion of ancient prophecy!"

There were more loud cheers. Catching the Skull Queen's eye, Obi-Wan protested, "You give me too much credit. It's not as if I found the power gems on my own."

"Ah, and he is modest too," the Skull Queen said. Raising her goblet again, she proclaimed, "In every way, he will make a perfect husband for the Skull Queen!"

The warriors roared even louder, but went silent as Calvaria stood and said, "No, Mother. The Jedi is to marry me!"

Obi-Wan looked at Calvaria, then to the Skull Queen, then back at Calvaria. The two women appeared quite serious. He turned to Bultar, who looked at him and blinked.

"I think I may laugh," Bultar said.

Obi-Wan warned, "Don't you dare!"

NEXT *STAR WARS* ADVENTURE:
THE HOSTAGE PRINCESS